H   M.M.S Re

cg Short's sweet   yes its OK C.E.B

MKW

J.P.

MM
Very good
short read!

mpH

Flanna

and the

Lawman

Flanna
and the
Lawman

Cathy Maxwell

THORNDIKE
CHIVERS

This Large Print edition is published by Thorndike Press®, Waterville, Maine USA and by BBC Audiobooks, Ltd, Bath, England.

Published in 2003 in the U.S. by arrangement with Harlequin Books S.A.

Published in 2003 in the U.K. by arrangement with Harlequin Enterprises II, B.V.

U.S. Hardcover 0-7862-5843-8 (Romance)
U.K. Hardcover 0-7540-5679-1 (Chivers Large Print)
U.K. Softcover 0-7540-5680-5 (Camden Large Print)

The text of this Large Print edition is unabridged.
Other aspects of the book may vary from the original edition.

Set in 16 pt. Plantin by Minnie B. Raven.

Printed in the United States on permanent paper.

British Library Cataloguing-in-Publication Data available

Library of Congress Cataloging-in-Publication Data

Maxwell, Cathy.
    Flanna and the lawman / Cathy Maxwell.
      p. cm.
    ISBN 0-7862-5843-8 (lg. print : hc : alk. paper)
    1. Women landowners — Fiction.   2. False personation —
Fiction.   3. Executions and executioners — Fiction.
4. Large type books.   I. Title.
PS3563.A8996F55 2003
813′.6—dc22   2003055457

For Helen Voigts

Dear Reader,

Have you ever met a man you thought you loved, but not enough to marry? Or so you told yourself?

I mean, you had your reasons for thinking the way you did at the time. Maybe you thought the two of you were too different. Your backgrounds weren't the same or you had different values. Maybe your family didn't like him. It's hard to choose between a man and your own blood. Maybe there were just things about him that irritated you. Chances are it was a combination of all the above.

However, later, when you *couldn't* go back, did dreams of him haunt your sleep? And in those quiet moments of the day did you ever fear that letting him go might have been the biggest mistake of your life?

Trace Cordell was that man for me.

And now I have a second chance.

Provided he isn't hanged from the gallows first!

Yours,

Fleana Kennedy

CHAPTER ONE

Trace Cordell stared ahead stoically determined to die better than he'd lived.

The ruddy-faced deputy serving as hangman set the noose around his neck. Trace wove to keep his balance, his hands tied tightly behind his back. His vision blurred as he looked out at the crowd of cattlemen, hired hands and local citizens gathered around the gallows built special in the middle of the street for his hanging. The prickly hemp of the new rope burned his skin and he could smell his own fear.

"Ex-Sheriff Cordell, do you have any *last* words you'd like to say?" Judge Rigby drawled from his front-row seat at the base of the gallows. The boys had brought out a table and chair from the saloon for the monkey-faced jurist to sit in comfort while he witnessed the hanging, a whiskey bottle in his right hand, a fat, half-smoked cigar in his left.

Trace shook his head. He couldn't answer. His throat was dry and there was a buzzing in his head right behind his eyes from a night of hard drinking.

Besides, what could he say he hadn't already in the kangaroo court they'd held minutes ago? He'd told the truth. He'd not remembered killing the man. That sometimes, lately, drink made him forget and lose time? Half the men in the crowd had the same problem, including the judge. The last thing Trace had remembered from the night before was the joy of being dealt a winning poker hand.

He woke to his own trial for murder.

"You've got nothing to say for your last words?" Rigby repeated as if he couldn't fathom such a thing. He pushed his bowler hat back from his forehead and looked over his shoulder at the crowd. "Doesn't seem right a man should pass from this life to the next without last words."

"How 'bout goodbye?" a cowpoke shouted.

"And good riddance?" another chimed in. The others laughed.

Rigby banged his bottle on the table for order. "We'll have some respect here. A man is about to die. And if he don't have anything to say, then as a fellow lawman, I think I will speak for him."

His audience groaned. Judge Rigby was a man who liked to hear himself talk. Well, he could talk until Doomsday as far as Trace was concerned, anything to put off the inevitable.

Carefully, the stubby judge placed the butt end of his cigar on the edge of the table and stepped up on the chair so he could best address the crowd. More than a bit tipsy himself, he had to hold the bottle out for balance. He removed his hat. The few strands of reddish hair on his bald pate stood straight up in the air like tiny flagpoles.

"Trace Cordell was at one time a good lawman. One of the best. Fierce and proud. We've all heard tales of him. But those who live by the sword will die by it and you other fellows out there better look at this man and heed the warning in your own lives." He nodded toward the broken door and glass windows of Birdie's Emporium, a saloon for the hard-bitten. "Justice is the rule of law, even for ex-lawmen and we don't ignore killing . . ." He then went off into a lecture about what makes a man a man in the West.

Trace stopped listening. Instead, he shifted his focus to the blueness of the sky that seemed to stretch out forever. The dry, ever present Kansas wind swirled around him, carrying with it pieces of dust and grit and the hint of summer heat.

He didn't want to die like this with his feet dancing on air and everyone watching. He'd seen too many men hanged not to know the indignities of this death.

And yet, he'd killed a man.

It wasn't as if he'd not killed before. As sheriff back in Loveless, he'd sent more than a dozen men to meet their Maker. But he could remember the look in their eyes, the determination in their faces. However, this man — ? No face formed in Trace's mind. His head throbbed harder the more he tried to remember. Whatever had happened was lost to him.

He wasn't a praying man, but a prayer formed in his mind. *Dear God, please, not like this.*

There was no answer. No clap of thunder. No giant hand coming down from the sky to save his unworthy soul.

He was going to hang.

Rigby wound up his eulogy by placing his hat on his head with a flourish and jumping down from the chair. He picked up his cigar butt, clamped it between his teeth and said, "Let's get on with it."

The crowd cheered.

Rigby's henchman tightened the noose around Trace's neck. "Won't be long now, Cordell." He gave Trace a friendly pat on the back and went down the steps to yank open the trap door beneath Trace's feet on command. Two other fellows stood ready and armed with shotguns in case Trace attempted to escape.

A preacher man stepped forward, opened his Bible, and began to recite some last words.

Trace saw some men remove their hats out of respect for the Good Book while others stepped forward for a better view of his death. He deliberately kept his mind blank. The pounding in his head increased.

Then, from the far corner of the crowd, he noticed movement. A woman in a straw bonnet worked her way forward, elbowing this man and that out of her way. She appeared anxious to get to the front row for his hanging.

The preacher finished. Rigby stood, his expression solemn. He raised his hand. "Now, with the power inves—"

The bonneted woman shouted, "Wait! Don't hang him! I saw what happened. Trace Cordell is innocent. He didn't shoot anyone." There was a hint of Irish in her voice, a voice Trace instantly recognized, and he groaned aloud.

Flanna Kennedy.

If his life was in her hands, he might as well step off the platform and hang himself.

She and her father had traveled Texas peddling rotgut in medicine bottles with enough charm and false promises to sweet talk a month's wages out of a saint. Trace had been forced to personally escort them out of Loveless. Unfortunately, that had been after they'd bled everyone dry and the reason for his carelessness was Flanna. He'd fallen in love with her. Head over heels. And that was the beginning of the end of his career as sheriff of Loveless.

Stood to reason he'd see her again with a noose around his neck.

Not that she didn't make a credible impression on his behalf. She was dressed for church, her straw bonnet trimmed in yellow ribbons and the blue of her sprigged calico dress the perfect match for her catlike eyes. Her hair was the vibrant strawberry-blond of the Irish and the few artful curls around her face caught and held the sunlight.

She even wore gloves. White leather ones. Obviously the year and a half since Trace had last seen her had been prosperous ones for Flanna.

He scanned the crowd searching for her rogue of a father. The overprotective Rory Kennedy was never far from his daughter. He wondered what game the old scoundrel was playing now.

Like so many others before him, Rigby fawned over Flanna's beauty. He pulled his hat off his head and slicked back his few hairs. A half dozen love-struck cowpokes did the same. "Miss Kennedy, we didn't know you were in town for the day."

Trace almost barked in surprised laughter at the respect in the judge's voice. Obviously he didn't know Flanna very well.

"I know who shot that man and it wasn't Sheriff Cordell," she said to Rigby in a breathless voice.

"*Ex*-sheriff," Rigby corrected with mild distraction, then said, "We've already had the trial."

"But you've had no justice."

The judge frowned. The crowd inched closer to hear better. Trace was listening especially closely, stunned by the revelation that he may not have committed the murder.

"How do you know who shot William Bates?" Rigby asked suspiciously.

"I was there at Birdie's," she confessed.

Now the idea of Flanna Kennedy patronizing a saloon did not surprise Trace at all . . . but apparently it did the good folks of Harwood. They acted like she was all milk and honey and not the stone-cold thief he knew.

A cowboy named Curly who had testified to the shooting murmured to his companions, "I would 'ave noticed her if she'd been here. Wouldn't 'ave been able to take my eyes off her." The others agreed.

"What *were* you doing there?" Rigby asked Flanna with interest. He dropped his cigar butt to the ground and pulled a fresh one from his suit coat. "Birdie's isn't the sort of place

for a fine young woman like yourself."

Trace almost choked. Rigby didn't
know Flanna at all.

"I came looking for Sheriff Cordell," she said. "I'd heard he was in
town and we had some, um, business
to attend between us. I saw everything that happened. I was standing
in the back room trying to manage a
way of catching Mr. Cordell's attention without drawing notice to myself
when the fight over a hand of cards
broke out."

Rigby clamped the unlit cigar in his
mouth, interested. "Go on."

Miss Kennedy continued. "The
gentleman who was killed —"

"Bates," the judge supplied.

"Yes, Mr. Bates. He pushed over
the card table and accused Mr.

Cordell of cheating, but before Mr. Cordell could speak, that gentleman with curly hair —"

"Curly?" Rigby asked. The cowhand of the same name stood close to the judge's elbow, a scowl on his face.

Flanna nodded. "Curly broke a chair over Mr. Cordell's head and knocked him out cold."

"Me?" Curly protested.

No wonder Trace's head hurt so bad.

"So if Cordell didn't shoot him, who did?" Rigby asked.

"Curly." She pointed a gloved finger right at him. "When Mr. Cordell went down, everyone started fighting save for Bates and Curly. Bates hurriedly grabbed up the money off the floor while Curly picked up Mr. Cordell's famous pearl-handled Colts. I thought it best to hide. No sense advertising my presence what with a group of wild men going at it. They were all acting like barbarians."

Several people nodded agreement.

"Curly and Bates ran for the back door where I was hiding," Flanna continued. "There they stopped and Curly demanded the money. Bates refused. They had angry words and Curly shot him. Bang! Just like that."

The accused cowhand doubled his fist. "I never did no such thing. Bill and I rode the trail together."

"But you never liked each other," a grizzled cowpoke pointed out.

"Yup, there was bad blood between them," said another.

"I liked him well enough," Curly shot back.

"Oh, yes," Flanna agreed. "You liked him enough to take the money. Then you went back into the saloon, and put the gun close to Mr. Cordell to make it look like his doing. I saw it all, you shot poor Mr. Bates right in the back."

During Trace's trial it was the shot in the back that had so many folks riled up. Flanna's comment spurred their sense of injustice.

For a moment Curly appeared ready to argue — and then he bolted for freedom, an action more telling than any admission of guilt. He was stopped by his compatriots before he'd taken three steps.

Rigby shouted for order. Curly shoved his way to toward the judge. "I had to shoot him," he told everyone. "He was stealing *our* money.

Just like she said."

"And what were *you* doing?" some-one challenged.

"I bet the money is in his saddle-bag," another answered. "He told me he was leaving town after he saw Cordell hang."

"Yeah, with our money!"

The call went out for someone to check Curly's horse and a party of men charged off to do exactly that.

Curly fell to his knees, shaking. He turned to the judge. "I didn't mean to shoot him. Just made me so mad he'd start a fight and then would try and steal it all. He was selfish that way."

Rigby answered by biting off the tip of the cigar and spitting it down at Curly. "You can tell me all about it later when I reconvene my court. Keep an eye on him, boys. I'll deal with him in a moment." He looked up at Trace. "Looks like what they say about you having nine lives is true, Cordell. Thanks to Miss Kennedy, you are going to walk. It's too bad. I was looking forward to hanging you."

"Maybe some other day," Trace said. And if he had his way, never. He couldn't wait to kick the dust of Harwood from his heels — especially now he knew Flanna was here. She may have saved his life, but he knew her too well. He wanted no part of Rory's schemes. The cost of the last one had been too high. "Someone get up here and cut my hands loose."

Rigby signaled his deputy to take care of the matter. The portly man climbed the stairs with obvious disappointment but did what he was told, slicing the ropes with a knife.

Meanwhile Rigby turned his full flirtatious attention on Flanna. "So, tell me, Miss Kennedy, why were you searching for Cordell last night?"

Yes, why was she? Trace wanted to pretend he wasn't interested in the answer, but he was. He rubbed his numb wrists. The pain of what felt like a thousand needles shot through them as his blood started circulating again. He couldn't even lift the noose from his neck.

Flanna hedged, apparently at a loss for words. "Why I was looking for him?" she repeated. Trace could see the wheels in her wily brain churning, and knew whatever she was about to say would be a lie. She'd never learn. She and her father were the devil's own playmates.

But even he, who knew her so well, was unprepared for what popped from her mouth.

"Oh, I was looking for him . . . because he's, um, he's my husband. Yes. He ran out on me almost two years ago and I've come to fetch him back."

Trace surged forward. "What a load of bull—" His words were cut off as the noose still around his neck pressed his windpipe.

CHAPTER TWO

Flanna ran to the edge of the gallows platform and gave Trace's leg a quick squeeze. As lies went, this wasn't a bad one. She gave him a pleading look. He had to go along with her on this. If anyone suspected she'd been searching for him because she needed a gunman, there would be hell to pay.

For a second, he stood stiff, his refusal clear in his distrustful eyes.

Please, she silently begged.

His gaze narrowed. He frowned. Then he stepped back, grabbed at the noose around his neck, and yanked it up over his head.

Flanna turned her attention back to the judge. "He's a little irritated about the hanging," she explained to her stunned audience.

"I didn't know you were married," Judge Rigby continued as if the fact he'd almost hanged an innocent man was of little importance. He put his hat back on his head. "If I'd known, I wouldn't have come courting."

"Well, Trace and I have one of *those* relationships."

The cowhands nodded. More than a handful of them had wives and sweethearts tucked away someplace, easily forgotten.

Trace came down the rickety stairs and to her side. He took her elbow, his grip tight. He was not in a good mood. "We'll be leaving now, *sweetheart*."

Judge Rigby blocked their way. "I just don't know why I wasn't told," he complained. "I mean, I used to sit on your doorstep and drink tea with you."

"I —" Flanna started, not certain what to say. Some men accepted gracefully their attentions were unwanted, while others, the tiresome ones, of whom Judge Rigby was one, always asked for an explanation. She'd never quite figured out how to let them down gently.

Her "husband" had no such pretense of manners. "You know how women are, Rigby. They either can't make up their minds or every other word out of their mouths is a lie."

"Yeah, that's right," Curly quickly seconded.

Trace sent him a look that could have crushed a rattler.

Flanna's temper flared at being publicly called a liar. "I'd forgotten what an arrogant bull you are —"

"Oh, what a tender reunion," Trace taunted. With a hard, steely glare of her own, she said succinctly, "A man whose wife just saved him from a noose around his neck had better watch his back."

Laughter broke out from the cowhands, as she'd known it would. She also knew the mighty Trace Cordell hated to be laughed at. She'd learned that little detail about him the hard way.

"You're not my w—"

Flanna cut him off, pleading her case directly to her small audience with a skillful weaving of truth and fiction. "My father never liked him. The two of them got in a terrible fight. You all knew how stubborn Rory could be. I was forced to choose between my father and Trace." She met his hard gaze. That was truth. But then, Trace had been the one to turn his back on her. Trace and his high-minded principles. Her father had warned her he would always be the lawman.

Except something about Trace had changed. She'd noticed it the night before.

Physically, he appeared the same: overlong straight dark hair that begged for a trim, silver eyes that could cut a person to pieces with a look, broad shoulders and slim hips. He seemed taller than she remembered, and harder. The lines around his eyes from the sun appeared deeper and his gaze lacked any of the warm humor he'd once possessed. Perhaps the change was the disreputable-looking two days' growth of beard on his jaw. Or the scent of hard liquor lingering on his skin.

Whatever the difference was, she sensed it went soul deep. This wasn't the Trace Cordell she'd once fallen in love with it. This was the sort of man no wise woman would ever trust.

But she had no choice.

"And you chose your father," Trace reminded her softly. "So that cuts me loose."

"Rory's dead," she said flatly. Grief welled inside her. For a second, she couldn't speak.

"Rory Kennedy dead?" Trace repeated with uncertainty. He glanced around as if expecting folks to contradict her. His grip on her arm softened and his hand came down to clasp hers. "I can't believe it. I thought the old rooster would live forever."

"He would have," Flanna said, unable to screen the bitterness from her voice, "if Burrell Slayton hadn't shot him."

Judge Rigby jumped into the discussion like the lapdog he was. "Here now. It was a hunting accident. We all know it was."

"Yes," she agreed, "except my father was the prey."

"There's no proof to your accusation, Miss Kennedy," Judge Rigby said evenly, then paused. His gaze shifted from her to Trace. "Or should I say, Mrs. Cordell?" he added thoughtfully. "You know, it's convenient of you to turn up married to one of the fastest guns in the West."

Panic rose in her throat, but Trace gave her hand a reassuring squeeze.

"Yes, it is," he agreed. "Wonder if Rory would have had his hunting accident if I'd been around."

"Can't say," Rigby replied. "Mr. Slayton had made his wants known. Old Rory didn't listen."

"I don't know if my hearing is any better."

The gauntlet had been thrown down. The cowboys shuffled back while Rigby's nervous hench- men edged closer. Their hands dropped to their guns.

Flanna stepped forward between them all. Her fight was with Burrell Slayton, not the judge. Trace would do her no good if he was shot before they left Harwood. "Come, Trace. Let me take you home. We need to talk." To her relief, he didn't argue, even while a few "wooo's" and catcalls met her words.

"I'll get my horse."

"Oh, your horse has been sold," Judge Rigby said, cockily hooking his thumbs in his suspenders.

"What?" Trace cocked his head as if he hadn't heard correctly.

The judge shrugged. "We had to pay for the damage to Birdie's saloon."

"And you thought it would be me?"

"We thought you'd be hanged," Judge Rigby answered. "A dead man doesn't need a horse."

His gallows humor drew a chuckle or two from the hard-bitten crowd gathered around but Trace obviously wasn't in the mood for jokes. He said quietly, "I want my horse."

"You can have it," the judge replied. "Your *wife* bought it."

Slowly, Trace turned to Flanna.

"You bought my horse?"

She was almost afraid to nod yes. "And your guns. And your hat. Everything is at the ranch. Well, except for the hat. I have it in the wagon."

"Good." He took her arm and turned her around. "Let's go get them and while we do that, I'm going to talk to you about taking your sweet time before speaking up. Five minutes later and I'd have been dancing on air."

"Well, I can explain."

"You are going to have a *lot* of explaining to do, *honey*."

"I hadn't expected them to charge you with the murder," she demurred.

"Mmm-hmm."

The cowboys and townsfolk moved out of their way but Judge Rigby's voice called them back. "Wait a minute, Cordell."

Trace turned. "What do you want now?"

"To give you advice. You know, Burrell Slayton isn't going to take well to the news you're married to Miss Kennedy."

"Who the hell is Slayton?"

"A man you don't want to cross. You might be wise to drift on."

Sliding a protective arm around Flanna's shoulders, Trace said, "And leave my wife?"

Rigby pushed back his bowler. "You already did once. 'Course I can't understand why any man would leave a woman like Miss Kennedy."

Trace's lips twisted into a smile. "Have you lived with her yet?" His quick rejoinder was met with a smattering of laughter.

The judge shook his head. "No,

something is wrong here." He waved his hands to include both Flanna and Trace. "This doesn't feel right. I don't know if I believe the two of you are married."

Before Flanna could protest, Trace asked, "Why should she lie?"

"She might have her reasons," the judge said, "reasons she'd best not pursue if she's smart." He put his cigar in his mouth. "After all, you two act like the furtherest thing from being loverly."

" 'Loverly'?" Trace's voice dropped to a deadly note. "I've had a chair broken over my head, spent the night in jail, almost got myself hanged . . . and now you are telling me I'm not *loverly* enough."

"The two of you act like strangers."

Flanna opened her mouth. "We

know each other well enough —" she started. But her words were cut off as Trace grabbed her arm, swung her around and, without warning, kissed her.

For a second she couldn't think. She couldn't move. Having been caught in midsentence, her mouth was still open and the kiss was awkward.

In spite of the vagrant life she'd led, her father had been overly protective. She'd allowed a few demure pecks on the cheek but nothing like having her mouth swallowed whole like this. And by the one man whose kisses she'd longed for.

Her heart pounded in her ears. Her eyes were open. Everyone was staring. Stiff and unnatural, she waved her arms in the air, not certain what to do with them.

Trace eased up slightly. The anger left him and his bruising lips softened, taking a more intimate turn.

Now, *this* was nice. With a soft sigh, Flanna closed her eyes and relaxed. His kiss became hungry and she couldn't help but taste him back.

Now she understood why everyone liked kissing so much. This was beyond pleasant. It made her vibrate with things she'd never felt with anyone else save him — need, desire, wanting.

She wrapped her arms around him. He responded by gathering her closer. His possessiveness sent a shiver of anticipation through her. But when his tongue stroked hers, she couldn't help a start of surprise . . . until she discovered she liked this.

He sucked lightly and she felt the

tug all the way to the deepest recesses of her woman's body — and she wanted *more.*

Time stood still. She lost all awareness. The dusty street, the watching crowd, even the earth beneath her feet faded from consciousness. Nothing existed save this kiss and the heady feeling of his hard body melding against hers. They fit perfectly like spoons. Her good bonnet fell back, the ribbon around her neck. Her hard, tight nipples pushed against his hard chest. His erection pressing between them gave evidence of his own reaction.

Dear God, she could kiss him all day —

Trace broke off the kiss. He stepped back and Flanna would have fallen to the ground, her legs unable to support her weight. He held her steady with an arm around her waist. "Satisfied?" he asked Judge Rigby.

The judge stared as slack-jawed as everyone else and Flanna realized she and Trace had given them quite a show. Rory must be turning in his grave!

A flood of heat burned her face. Self-consciously she fussed with her bonnet, attempting to set herself back to rights.

Trace smiled at the judge. "We'll be leaving. Flanna and I have some *unfinished* business to attend to."

Low whistles and jostling met his proclamation. Judge Rigby didn't say a word, but Flanna could feel his hard gaze on them as she and Trace headed for the wagon parked in front of the Mercantile.

He helped her into the seat without

a word, then climbed up beside her. She reached for the reins but his hand covered hers. His eyes were like slivers of ice. She wondered what he was thinking.

"I'll drive," he said.

She nodded and sat back. With a whack of the reins, he started the horse forward, heading out of town. The judge, his compatriots and the small crowd followed their every movement.

Within moments they were alone. Trace drove in silence until they were a good mile away from Harwood. He stopped the wagon.

"Now what the hell is going on?"

His expression was anything but *loverly*.

CHAPTER THREE

"They shot him," Flanna said, the corners of her mouth tight, her eyes bright. "He was unarmed, Trace. He went to talk to Slayton, to work out a compromise, and they shot him cold. They didn't even bring him back to me but buried him in Harwood quick as a cat can blink."

Surprisingly, grief washed over him. There'd been no love lost between himself and the wily Irishman. As her father, Rory had believed no man was good enough for his daughter in spite of his own two-bit swindles and petty schemes. He'd flat-out told Trace that when Flanna married it would be to a better man than some whore's son who'd made a name for himself with a gun — even if he was a lawman.

Trace had countered he didn't know how Rory thought he was going to meet such a man for his daughter while peddling rotgut disguised as medicinal tonic and getting thrown out of every town they drove through. He had as much right to Flanna as anyone.

Besides, Flanna loved him . . . or so he had thought.

In the end, Rory had proved him wrong. She'd left with her father without a backward glance.

Still, Trace hadn't wished the rascal dead.

"I warned him," he said tightly. "I told Rory he'd better change his ways or someone would put a bullet through him."

Her gaze hardened. "He did change, Trace. After we left Loveless . . ." Her voice trailed off. She turned her attention to the line of the far horizon beyond the green prairie of the high plains. "After we left Loveless," she began again, "I told him I didn't want to live that way anymore. I thought about what you'd said, about how out here in the West a person could have a second chance to be whatever he or she wanted to be. No past, no regrets. Just move on and make yourself into someone new, someone meaningful." She swung her gaze to him. "Do you remember?"

He'd always talked that way. It had been his "sheriff" sermon, his friendly advice to those on the wrong path. The words sounded foreign to him now. "Yeah."

She crossed her arms tight against her middle. "After . . . after what happened between us, when we parted —"

"Oh, you mean you've finally remembered we are *not* married?"

Her hesitation evaporated at his sarcasm. "I had to cobble together a story for why I was searching for you. I couldn't let Judge Rigby be thinking I wanted you to bring Slayton to justice. They're all afraid of him and his friends."

"But to claim we're *married?*" He shook his head. "That was more than a bald-faced lie, Flanna. It was —" It was what? An insult? An injury? A reminder of what he couldn't have?

"I hated choosing between the two of you, but he was my father. You couldn't have expected me to turn my back on him?"

Yes, he had. "You can skip the explanations." He swung his gaze away from her, preferring the ruts in the dirt road to the face of the woman he'd once loved. "Anything between us is in the past. I've managed fine without you." He started to pick up the reins but her tart words stopped him.

"Yes, I can see you have. When did you last shave, Trace? Or bathe? You smell of the bottle."

"I'm sorry, m'lady, but I've spent the night in jail, I was almost hanged, otherwise I would have taken a perfumed bath for you. Eau de lilies."

"I doubt that. The high-and-mighty Sheriff Cordell doesn't put himself out for anyone. It's his way or no way."

"I would have married you," Trace charged. "I offered you everything I had, but it wasn't enough."

"Aye, and you would have reminded me every day of what *grand* favor you did not throwing me out of town," she replied. "Rory warned me. He said you were too self-righteous. A prig."

"He called me a pig?" Anger felt good. Anger offered protection.

"Not a pig," she corrected, her Irishness coming out. "A *prig*. You ken? A sanctimonious, rigid, know-it-all who must have his own way."

"If you felt that way, why didn't you let me hang?" He'd almost prefer hanging versus sitting here in the sun taking a tongue-lashing off the one woman he'd ever wanted and couldn't have.

"Because I need you," she told him bleakly. "No one else will help me. They're all afraid of Slayton. And then, just when I was ready to give up, I heard from a passing neighbor that the great Sheriff Cordell was sitting in Harwood playing cards. It was an omen, Trace. God sent you here to help me."

"God had nothing to do with it." He slapped the horse with the reins. "I was passing through and I'm going to keep moving, Flanna. I'm not looking for any fights. I've had enough."

"You'll change your mind once you hear my story," she insisted stubbornly.

He ignored her.

"Besides, it's all your fault."

He held his tongue.

She glanced his way and then added, "If not for you, Rory would still be alive."

Temper seared through him. Trace pulled the wagon to a halt. He faced her. "How do you figure that?"

With a haughty lift of her stubborn chin, she said, "Because we wouldn't even be here if it wasn't for you. I didn't want to wander aimlessly anymore. I wanted a home, honest work, and a place that I could put down roots. Have you ever wanted such a thing?"

Yeah, he had. With her. "So what did Rory do, swindle this Slayton out of land and earn a bullet for his efforts?"

Anger flashed in her eyes. "No. We decided to change our lives just like you advised, *Sheriff*. Rory bought this parcel of land from a man who was selling and we decided to change who we were. We're ranchers now and doing well even in such a short time. We have fifty head of cattle."

Trace didn't like hearing she was fine without him. His life hadn't been worth a damn since she walked out. "So what did happen? What did Slayton have against Rory?"

"Nothing against him. He wanted what Rory had — water. Here on the high plains, water is like gold. The parcel we bought has a stream that runs right into the Cimarron and a spring that bubbles with the sweetest water you can ever imagine."

"Sounds like a prime stake."

"It is. And Slayton wants it. He needs the water for his herds. Turns out the man we'd bought it from had been chased out by Slayton's threats, but Rory was not one to run, especially since we were making a good go of it." She placed her hand on Trace's arm. "I have a rage in me for vengeance that could shake the heavens. Rory was no saint, but he didn't deserve to die like that, either. Slayton expects me to sell, but I won't. He'll have to kill me to for my land. And that's why I need you. You are a man of justice. You'll stop Slayton."

That's why I need you. Trace dropped his gaze to her fingers on his arm . . . and he wanted to be her hero.

Yup, the time had come to leave.

"Didn't you hear Rigby?" he asked. "I'm an *ex*-lawman. I'm not the sheriff of Loveless anymore."

She drew back as if first hearing the news. "You left Loveless? I can't believe such a thing. You were the pillar of that town. Everyone respected you."

"Respected me enough to give me the boot." He couldn't look at her. Instead, he drove the horse forward. Better to get where they were going so he could leave.

Flanna sat in stunned, gratifying silence. It lasted only a moment. "Why would the people of Loveless do that? You took that town from a wild cattle stop to a thriving village."

He focused on the road ahead. "Well, a good number of folks were upset that you and Rory had separated them from their hard-earned cash."

"We *sold* those bottles to them and we never asked for more than what a person was willing to pay."

"You also made some promises about the elixir."

"It does what we promised," she told him primly. "If a person is in the proper frame of mind. You have to work with it to make the magic happen." She paused. "Turn here and follow this trail over beyond that ridge." She sat back. "So why did they really ask you to leave?"

"Because times are changing," Trace said dully. "A man who has killed as often as I have is not suited for the kind of town Loveless had become. They have churches there now and stores, families."

"You do have a reputation."

"And how did I earn it?" He swore softly. "I gave them everything I had. When there was fighting to do, I did it. I took the town back from the

Watkins gang and I kept it. I made something of myself in Loveless. Because of my *reputation* as a gunfighter, the streets were safe. There was law. And then, some medicine man comes through and people start to think I don't fit the town anymore."

They'd also remembered about his being born a bastard. Most of them had known his mother. Hell, years ago, she'd been a cornerstone of the community in spite of her trade. Of course, with civilization, people's opinions changed. "They started thinking they wanted a better man. So they hired some policeman from the east and wished me well. They even asked me to leave."

Bitter humiliation and injustice choked him. And it had all started with her. Before she'd come, everyone had liked him fine. Of course, he'd known his place back then. He'd never have courted a town gal, but Flanna's love had let him believe he was one of them.

God, he wished he had a drink!

Flanna sat quietly. He didn't look at her. He hated himself this way . . . and he didn't want pity. Especially hers. He'd make his way. One way or the other.

But he was tired. Damn tired . . .

"I have your guns. And your horse."

He glanced at her. He couldn't tell what she was thinking. But there was no pity. "When we get to your place, I'll pick them up and be off."

She didn't answer but leaned forward, placing her hand right beside his thigh on the hard, wood seat. Another half inch over and she'd touch him.

Every fiber of his being honed in on that one tantalizing possibility . . . especially after that kiss back in Harwood.

"I need you."

Her throaty words stirred his imagination.

"I did love you," she added. "It was like cutting out my heart to leave you, but I couldn't abandon my father, and the two of you were oil and water."

He tightened his grip on the reins. The trail across the prairie curved, disappearing into the high grass. He could feel her watching him.

"You could start new, too," she offered. "Just as Rory and I did."

Trace didn't answer. That had

been his advice for others, not himself.

At last, she sat back. "What shall I do about Slayton?"

"I'd sell. You know how to drive a hard bargain." There, he'd absolved himself of responsibility.

"And what? Move on from the first home I've known?"

He chose his words deliberately. "You're good at moving on, Flanna. You won't have any problems at all."

She crossed her arms. There was a beat of silence and then she said, "Rory was right — you can be a bastard, Trace Cordell."

"That's what they tell me," he replied grimly.

As if sensing the tension, the horse picked up his pace. "We're almost home," Flanna said.

"Ah, yes. Kennedy's paradise," Trace countered.

She didn't reply. At the same moment the trail took them up over a bluff — and there it was.

The horse lifted his head and whinnied, an announcement he was home. An answering call came from Trace's horse, Bill, down in a makeshift corral.

Trace felt a stab of disappointment.

The homestead — a soddy and a barn a little larger than a stable — was like a hundred others he'd seen across the prairie. He hadn't really known what to expect. Something in Flanna's tone when she'd spoken of the place had made him picture grandeur on a scale that common sense told him couldn't be found in Kansas. But he wasn't expecting a soddy. He hated the small houses made out of blocks of tough sod. They smelled of earth and the stories he'd heard of snakes put a shudder through him. Even the barn, really nothing more than a lean-to, had sod walls. A chicken coop with some of the sorriest-looking poultry he'd ever seen had been built against the barn.

A line of huge cottonwoods, locust trees, and hedges marked the path of the stream. There was water in the air. He could smell it. He knew many ranchers would kill for this parcel of land.

"Isn't it wonderful?" Flanna said proudly. She reached for the reins.

"It's something," he agreed truthfully.

"We started with nothing, not even the sod house."

"You made money fast."

She bit back a smile. "Well, we had that bit of a stake we'd earned in Loveless."

"Oh, yes, *that*," he replied dryly, and she wisely let the matter rest.

She drove down the bluff into the yard. Two hound dogs of dubious heritage barked a warning and then jumped up into the wagon to jubilantly greet their mistress. They even had some slobber for Trace.

Flanna laughed at their happy eagerness. "Calm down," she ordered, removing her straw bonnet and holding it high so the dogs wouldn't get it. Immediately, the ever present wind captured her red-gold hair and playfully lifted it in the breeze. She jumped down before Trace could offer a hand. "Let me put this horse up and I'll show you around the place."

Trace thought he could see everything from where he sat. His buckskin, Bill, came to the edge of the corral where Flanna had him penned and nickered.

Flanna's laughing gaze met Trace's. "Your horse is a bit of a stud. He has his eye on my Spice."

"Well, he'd best be thinking about leaving," Trace said, and the smile disappeared from her face.

"Yes. Of course."

He told himself he had no reason to feel like a deserter. There were no promises between them. Flanna shouldn't have assumed. Still . . . even the dogs seemed to look at him with recriminations.

"Here, you go put your bonnet

away before the dogs eat it and I'll see to Spice," he offered as penance. In truth, his conscience was bothering him, but he knew about battles over land. Where money was involved, some men were ruthless. Flanna would be safer selling and starting anew somewhere else.

She nodded and hurried inside. He'd just finished unharnessing the horse when she returned. She held his guns and holster in her hand. "I thought you'd want these."

He stared at the pearl handles of his guns and felt a sudden unease. What good had these guns ever done him? This morning he'd woke thinking he'd killed a man. He took a step back. "Set them up on the wagon," he said, turning away. "I'll get them later."

If Flanna noticed a change in him, she gave no indication. Instead she said, "Let Spice graze. She'll not wander far. I want to show you something." Without waiting for his response, she turned and walked toward the stream.

"It won't do any good," he called after her. He waited. She kept walking. "Flanna, I'm not staying. I'm not your hero."

She stopped, turned. "Are you coming?"

"You told me no once. I'm not some lapdog to hang around."

She kept walking. "You made yourself perfectly clear. You'll not champion my battle. But I want you to see this, to understand why I won't go without a fight. Wait until you see what I want to show you."

His feet started moving. He didn't know why, but he didn't stop himself.

She led him down by the stream and then turned with a smile. "What do you think?"

On a level bit of land along the banks of the stream stood the foundations of a house. The first floor had been built with supporting beams set in. To his right was a stack of lumber for building, almost as high as his chest.

"It's not much now," she told him. "Rory and I sketched it in a bit on the ground and had been working on it as we got a chance. Wood is expensive, but we want the best. We already have the glass windows. They arrived in Dodge the day after they shot my father."

She stepped up on the boards. "I

68

wanted it by the stream so we'd have its music in the morning. Rory wanted a big porch so he could sit in his chair in the evenings and enjoy the shade. In the summer, this is the only place to catch a breeze." She ran her hand over a piece of rough wood, her expression wistful. "I can't give it up. I've been traveling since I was a wee thing. This is my first home. I'll never sell. Can you understand now how I feel?"

Oh, yes, he could. Her eyes were shiny with pride and the wind blew her curls around her face. He felt a need the likes of which he'd never experienced before. For her.

This was Flanna, he reminded himself. She was a tease, a lure used by her father to turn men's minds from his true purpose. And she'd been very

69

good at ensnaring him. She'd cost him everything he'd valued — his position as sheriff, his pride . . . and in turn had spurned his love.

"I want you to stay." Her husky voice cut through his doubts. Her gaze slid from his as if she found the words difficult to say. "I need you."

She knew how to twist him in knots.

Trace took a step back, and then another. "I don't know how you do it, but you have the touch."

Flanna stiffened. "What do you mean?"

"You know exactly what you're doing. It's as if you are trying to grab my soul. Well, it won't work, not this time. I thank you for saving my life, but, lady, we're through."

He turned to walk away just as the

dogs began barking. Riders were coming over the bluff. "Do you know them?" he asked Flanna.

"Yes." Her mouth flattened. "It's Burrell Slayton and his men. Well, it appears you are going to be making his acquaintance, after all. Shall I invite them for tea?" She didn't wait for an answer but walked forward to greet her "guests."

CHAPTER FOUR

Slayton rode on a white horse at the head of a small party of rough-looking men.

Her heart pounding in her ears, Flanna stopped in the middle of the yard waiting for him to come to her. Trace had followed, and now stood no more than five feet away, his expression wary.

Her pride refused to drag him into a fight he did not want. But his refusal to help her cause hit her full-force. She'd counted on his help. From the moment she'd heard he was in town, she'd known he'd been sent to help her . . . and she'd thought she'd have a second chance at his love. Leaving him had been a mistake.

Now, she knew she was alone. The Trace who stood behind her wasn't the man she remembered. That man had an inborn sense of justice. He'd have fought for what was right regardless of the circumstances.

This man thought only of himself.

She directed her resentment toward her unwanted guests.

Dust swirled around the hooves of the horses as Slayton called his band to a halt ten feet from where she stood. "Miss Kennedy," he greeted with jovial humor. He was a lean man, fastidious in dress and manner — especially when compared to the coarse men riding with him. His boots were polished to a shine the trail could never dull, his shirt, a crisp white against the black of his jacket, and his ribbon tie made him appear as if he'd just come from church.

Rory had always liked the vain. He claimed they were the easiest marks. For that reason, he'd assumed he could handle Slayton. He hadn't expected to be shot.

"Or should I say, *Mrs. Cordell?*" Slayton queried in soft, polite tones, leaning one lazy arm over his saddle horn. His gaze moved past her to where Trace stood, a silent witness. "How convenient for you to turn out to be married to one of the fastest guns in the West. I'm surprised Rory didn't brag about it."

"What do you want?" she demanded.

Slayton grinned. "I want what I've always wanted, Mrs. Cordell. I want to buy your property. I was hoping I could have a word with your *husband* about the matter."

Too late, Flanna realized the short-coming of her marriage scheme. By law, a wife's property belonged to her husband. Trace's advice for her to sell rang in her ears. She blocked his path. "It's not for sale. It'll *never* be for sale. Not to you."

"That's all well and good, Mrs. Cordell," Slayton replied, "but I'd like to hear from your husband. This is men's business now."

"How much are you offering?" Trace's rough voice cut right to her soul.

Slayton's teeth flashed in triumph. "Three hundred dollars. Gold."

"Only three hundred?" Trace repeated.

The smile on Slayton's face flattened. "My price is more than generous."

"I have another price in mind." Trace came up to stand by Flanna. "How about admitting to the murder of Rory Kennedy?"

Flanna's heart gave a glad leap. Burrell Slayton sat up on his horse, his lazy good humor gone. The riders behind him tensed.

"I didn't have anything to do with Rory's accident. I wasn't even close to where it happened."

"You were the last person to see him," Trace replied evenly. "If you didn't shoot him, you know who did."

Slayton's eyes turned cold. "I had nothing to do with Kennedy's death, Cordell."

"Well, naming the killer is my price for this land."

Flanna linked her arm in Trace's. She saw the trap he'd laid. Slayton could never admit to the murder. And if he turned in one of his own men, well, there was no doubt in her mind the killer would squeal like a cowardly dog to save his own neck.

"You are making a mistake, Cordell," Slayton said. "A fatal one if you continue to accuse me of something I didn't do." The three men behind him shifted their hands to their guns.

Trace didn't waver. "Threats won't get you what you want."

"I don't make threats. I make promises."

Flanna clenched her fists, but Trace smiled easily. "Any time you want to carry out a *promise,* you go right ahead. I'm not Rory Kennedy. I know how to watch my back."

"We'll see." Slayton nodded to his men and, with a sharp jerk of the reins, turned his horse around. But as he passed one of his men, Flanna caught a signal pass between them.

"Watch out," she warned Trace even as the man pulled his gun and fired.

The bullet whizzed into the dirt right at the toe of Trace's boot. Flanna gave a small yelp of surprise and jumped back, but Trace didn't flinch.

Instead, a change seemed to come over him. His eyes took on a blazing light. He actually seemed to grow in stature. He looked up at the man who had shot at him, a trail-beaten cowboy with a toothless grin, still proudly holding the gun on him.

In two giant, quick steps, Trace was in front of him. He grabbed the cowhand by the front of his shirt and yanked him off his horse as if he weighed no more than a rag doll. His movements had been so unexpected, the man hadn't had the presence of mind to shoot.

Trace knocked the gun from his hand. It flew through the air to land close to Flanna who promptly snatched it up.

Wrapping both hands around the cowboy's neck, Trace held him high. The man's face started to turn red, his mouth gaped for breath. His comrades pulled their guns. Her knees shaking, Flanna trained the gun on them.

Trace ignored them all. He acted possessed, his focus was on the cowboy who struggled for breath. "If you ever take another shot at me, you'd better not miss," he said in a low, dangerous voice Flanna had never heard from him before. "Because if you do, the next time, I'll kill you."

The cowboy's feet were kicking out now, trying to swing free of Trace's dangerous grip. Then Trace let him go. The cowpoke fell to the ground, his legs unable to support his weight. On all fours, he started hacking, trying to catch his breath.

Trace pinned Slayton with his hard gaze. "Leave Flanna alone. I'll not let harm come to her."

Slayton's lips formed a firm line as if he bit back a retort. Instead, he looked at the two remaining men. "Pick Tom up. Let's get out of here."

He rode off while his men scurried to obey under Trace's watchful eye.

One caught Tom's horse while the other rode over and held down a hand. Tom took a minute before he could gather enough strength to reach up for help. His burly friend swung him up behind his saddle and the trio followed their boss.

Flanna watched until they had gone over the bluff and out of sight. Any triumph she felt was tempered by the swift, controlled violence of Trace's actions. Tom could have shot him. And yet Trace's reaction had unsettled her. The way he had walked into the line of the cowboy's gun had been suicidal and yet Trace had not hesitated. Something dangerous and unrestrained had overtaken him. Something she didn't understand.

But she could appreciate why the people of Loveless had asked him to move on. And her own father's doubts. Slowly, she turned to face him and what she saw almost broke her heart.

He studied some point on the ground, a statue of a man made of muscle and flesh. His shoulders were hunched in thought and deep lines etched his face. She wondered what he was thinking . . . and knew the answer.

He hated what he had become. She understood as if she could read his mind.

Immediately she stepped forward. "You were wonderful," she whispered. "You were like the archangel Michael with his avenging sword. The way you walked right into the gun sight and grabbed that cowboy by the neck." She hooked her arm in his. "The man was quivering with fright and his friends were, too."

Trace watched her, silent.

His quietness made her uneasy. "You did it," she assured him. "Slayton will think twice before crossing you."

"He'll be back. And when he comes, he'll bring more men. I've challenged him. It's personal now."

His words sobered her. "Why do you say that?"

"Because I know his kind. Hell, I *am* his kind."

"No, you're not." She gave his arm a squeeze, feeling the hard muscle there. "You're a good man, a brave one. You're no more like him than a Thoroughbred is like a burro."

"Yeah." He turned from her, but she drew her hand down his arm to capture his hand.

He looked at her, expectant. When they stood this close, she was so aware of him, of his size, of those hard silver eyes, of the long, tapered fingers rough with calluses.

Merciful God, she was still in love with him.

She thought she'd been over him but then there'd been the kiss . . . and all the arguing . . . and then the confrontation with Slayton —

She dropped his hand as if it had turned into a burning ember.

He noticed and he didn't like it. "What's the matter?" he said carefully.

Her stomach did a nervous twist. She wasn't about to admit her feelings. He wouldn't believe her even if she did. He was not the kind of man who gave second chances. "Nothing. I'm, uh —" Words failed her, especially under his scrutiny. She attempted to recover. "What are you going to do now?"

"Stay and fight." He walked toward Spice, grazing by the wagon. He took the horse by the mane and guided it toward the barn.

Flanna took after him, skipping to catch up. Placing a hand on his arm, she made him stop. "Listen, Trace, this isn't your fight. Maybe I was wrong to draw you in."

His brows lifted in surprise. "You should have thought about that before you claimed to be married to me. Everyone thinks I own the land, Mrs. Cordell."

"Well . . . yes. But you were going to leave."

"I changed my mind."

She glanced at the creek where the water merrily rushed over stones. The precious, precious water. "I just don't want anything to happen to you." And it would. A sense of impending gloom seemed to hover over her. Perhaps she *should* sell.

"Besides, maybe I like being married."

"Like it?" She looked up, startled. The expression on his face was indiscernible . . . until his gaze lowered . . . down to her breasts with raw, hungry desire.

The air crackled with tension.

Flanna didn't dare move. She could barely breathe. Her breasts seemed to fill and tightened. An edgy tingling danced across her skin to settle deep inside her.

And yet the sun was still shining, birds whistling, and the ground was still beneath her feet. The horse nudged Trace as if to tell him to get moving. He let go of the animal and took a step closer, raising his gaze to linger on her lips.

She cleared her throat and then edged back. "But we aren't married."

He smiled.

"I told you earlier I'm willing to pay you for your help," she said stiffly.

"Like a *hired* hand?" he asked softly, his inflection giving the offer a meaning she hadn't intended.

Again she cleared her throat, surprised at how nervous she was. "Yes. Fair's fair."

He nodded as if in agreement. "Well now, what is a 'fair' price?"

Flanna forced herself to pretend

she wasn't aware of how tall he was, how intimidating . . . or how easy it would be to step into his arms. "I did save your life."

He laughed. His chest so close, she could feel the heat from his body. "Yes, you did. Shame you didn't make it for the trial."

"But I was there in time to stop the hanging." Her voice sounded as if she'd run a great distance and she was starting to feel lightheaded. Maybe now was a good time to put a little distance between them. But as she started to back away, his hand caught her arm — just as it had in town before he'd kissed her.

"My services don't come cheap, *Mrs.* Cordell."

Her toes curled at his use of her fake married name. His voice was laden with unspoken promises. "I didn't think they did." She struggled for sanity. This was a bargain they were driving. She must keep her wits. "I'll offer you ten dollars a day."

He laughed.

Annoyed, she retorted, "It's a fair price. More than you earned as sheriff."

"And how did you come by that sort of cash? From the people of Loveless?"

A guilty heat stole across her cheeks. "By the look of you, you shouldn't be turning up your nose at the offer of a little cash."

"No, I shouldn't, should I? Especially covered in trail dust." He pulled her closer, the light of a hundred devils gleaming in his eyes. "And it has been a while since I've had a good meal or other —" he gave her arm a gentle squeeze "— comfort."

Comfort. Oh dear. "What are you thinking?" she asked, cautious and yet so very aware of his legs now pressed against hers.

"That perhaps I might take you up on the offer you made in town."

"Which offer?" she squeaked.

Again, his gaze flicked over her breasts. "About being a wife."

Flanna's mouth went dry. "I was . . . saving you . . . when I made that claim," she explained faintly. Good Lord, she could barely think. Or move her gaze from his mouth. She'd always known Trace was a fine-looking man but she'd never noticed how sensual his lips were. Manly lips. The kind of lips that had proved they knew how to kiss.

He grinned, his white teeth in his whiskered face giving him a roguish look. "Well, that's the price, Flanna. You wanted to pretend to be my wife in Harwood. The way I see it, we don't have any other choice but to continue the game."

For a second, the need, the desire, the wanting of him made it difficult for her to reason. Rory would never have approved. But Rory wasn't here.

"This is a Philistine's bargain," she whispered.

"You've struck that kind of a bargain before." He smiled. "It all depends on what you want." His lips mere inches from hers, he said, "It's what *I* want."

Merciful heavens, this was the devil's own pact. Her traitorous body yearned for his body heat. She loved the feeling of his arms around her. He made her feel protected and safe.

"I have needs, Flanna," he said, his voice close to her ear going straight through to her heart. "Needs only a wife can provide."

She made a small sound of distress that sounded embarrassingly like a whimper of desire. "A pretend wife?"

His lips brushed the top of her forehead. "Oh, yes. But a wife in *every* way."

Flanna feared she'd swoon. Rory must be rolling in his grave. Almost as if in a trance, she nodded. "Done."

"Good."

Then to her surprise, he started to remove his shirt.

She looked around wildly. It was broad daylight, no later than midafternoon. He couldn't be thinking of ravishing her now? "Wait. Trace, what are you doing?" His bare chest was rock-hard with muscle. His shoulders made others appear puny. "Oh, my," she murmured, part in distress and part in admiration. She fluttered a hand up to her collar, the heat of the day suddenly overwhelming. "I mean, you can't — I can't — We should at least go inside —"

He cut her off by tossing his dirty, sweat-stained shirt in her face. "Here."

Gagging, she removed the shirt. "What is this for?"

"It needs washing. I've got another in my saddlebags. Best get busy —" He paused and added with smug emphasis, *"Wife."*

Laughing, he drove Spice into the barn.

CHAPTER FIVE

Trace congratulated himself as he walked the mare into the barn. *Finally,* he'd gotten a bit of his own back over Flanna. She'd thought he was after something else. The expression on her face when he'd taken off his shirt had been comical. And then, when he'd thrown the shirt at her — *ha!* He'd made her feel like a fool. Just as she'd made him feel back in Loveless.

No sir, she hadn't liked that. Even now she stood holding his shirt away from her as if she'd rather burn than wash it.

But she wouldn't because for once in her life, she needed him.

Trace put Spice in a roped-off stall.

Outside, Bill ran around the corral, wanting attention. Or, more likely, company.

The barn itself was a small, low-roofed soddy. Rory had put every inch of space to use. Hanging from the rafters were tools. A plow rested in the corner. A row of bulging sacks were stacked against the wall. Trace wandered over and knelt to investigate. Wheat seed. He'd heard it grew well in these parts. Of course, the seed should have been planted weeks ago . . . round about the time Rory had been shot.

The lucky Irish bastard. He'd had it all. Land, a future, and a daughter who loved him.

"Perhaps I deserved that."

He turned at the sound of Flanna's crisp voice. She stood a few steps from him, his shirt in her clenched hands, her face pinched. The air in the stable grew close. Too close. He shrugged.

She interpreted his gesture accurately. "You don't want to talk about it, do you? Every time I bring up what happened between us you grow angry and push me away."

He stood, unexpectedly ill-at-ease at being half naked in front of her. What was it about Flanna that made him feel more like an awkward boy instead of a man? It was as if she could see to the heart of his black soul. His saddle and saddlebags were stacked on top of several others draped over a makeshift sawhorse close to the grain bags. He reached into his bag and pulled out his other shirt, giving her his back. It wasn't much cleaner than the one she held. "Forget it. Loveless was a long time ago."

"I feel like it all happened yesterday." When he didn't speak, she said, "I didn't mean for things to get as tangled up the way they did."

He didn't want this conversation. He pulled his shirt over his head.

"Trace —" she started, and suddenly he'd had enough.

"I'm here, dammit," he swore. "You wanted my help. You have it. Leave the past where it is."

"I can't. I *loved* you."

For a heartbeat he couldn't breathe. He couldn't think.

And then he remembered.

"Damn, you are good." He tucked his shirt into his pants, his movements jerky . . . and he hated himself because he wanted to believe. She was so lovely, so tempting, and yet —

"You've said those words before, Flanna. They come easy to your lips, especially when you want something. Well, the blinders are off. I'm not the moony-eyed —" He caught himself in time. He'd been about to say "lonely." He wasn't the moony-eyed, lonely man he'd been in Loveless.

But that wasn't true, was it?

He turned and his gaze dropped again to the sacks of seed.

He sensed her take a step toward him. "You feel I betrayed you," she said.

He remained silent . . . and so very aware of her.

"If I'd thought things could have been different, I'd never have left. But Rory and I milked your town dry,

Trace. I wanted to stop, but it was too late and you wouldn't have forgiven me. You still won't." She paused, cleared her throat. "Rory said a man like you didn't forgive easy."

She moved closer until she stood right at his arm. He could feel the heat of her body. When he'd first met her, he remembered thinking she'd smelled like fresh grass on a spring day. New and green, vital, inviting. Now the scent of her filled him. It would be so easy to put his arms around her. To kiss her as he had in town but with deeper intent.

Ah, yes, that kiss had been a mistake.

"You said a person can make herself into whatever she wants to be out here. No matter what her past was. Were you lying to me, Trace? Because I've tried. I am different. Wiser."

The light lilt of her voice wrapped itself around him. He struggled to protect himself. "Maybe I was wrong. Maybe a person can't change."

"Or maybe you are fooling yourself," she countered. "Especially if you think answers can be found in a whiskey bottle."

He hated the way she shot right to the heart of a matter. She'd never been one to sugar the truth . . . and if the truth be known, he was starting to feel embarrassed. Perhaps he had over-reacted when they'd thrown him out of Loveless. He'd never been one to feel sorry for himself and yet, here he was.

Damn Flanna. She had a talent for making him see the truth in himself.

He walked over to where a coil of rope hung from the ceiling. "I've got work to do if I'm going to be ready for Slayton when he comes."

Flanna recognized that she had been dismissed. Trace didn't want to talk . . . but then he'd always been a man of few words. However, she sensed he wasn't as indifferent to her as he wished her to believe.

And she wasn't about to leave him be. She'd made the mistake of leaving him once. She'd not do it again.

"What do you have planned?" she asked.

He stiffened, a frown coming to his lips.

"After all, we're partners," she explained, her woman's intuition telling her she must keep herself in front of

101

him. No matter how angry he got, she didn't dare let him turn his back on her. Because she knew now what she wanted — she wanted him.

"I should know what you are planning so I can help."

His irritation plain, he replied, "I have it handled."

"Of course you do," she agreed diplomatically, "but I need know what you expect me to do."

"You don't have to do anything," he said pointedly.

Flanna sensed she'd best not push him. "Ah, then, I'll be fixing the supper. And washing your shirt."

He glanced at her as if he thought she teased him with her abrupt capitulation. She kept her expression carefully neutral.

"What is going through your

scheming Irish mind, Flanna?"

"You give me too much credit, Trace. All I'm trying to do is protect what is mine against Slayton." She moved now, deliberately walking close as she passed him. "I'll be in the house, being a good *wife*."

He shifted at her emphasis of the title, wary as if expecting her to pounce on him. Giving Spice's nose a rub as she passed, she asked with studied nonchalance, "So what are you planning to do with the rope? Build a fence?"

She was teasing but he said seriously, "Yes. They may come back tonight. I'll run this rope through the trees by the creek to create a barricade."

"That won't stop a band of armed men," she replied.

"No, but the horses will be confused when they hit the rope. They'll balk, maybe even bolt. Slayton's men are cowards at heart. They get the courage from their numbers. And they are lazy. If the horses act up, if this job looks like the least bit of work, they'll run." He yanked the end of the rope taut. "Then it will just be Slayton and me."

"What about the bluff?"

He smiled, more relaxed now they were discussing something other than their disturbing history. "I'll build a quick fence from the wood Rory has stored for the house. Again, something that will startle the horses. And I'd best get started. We have less than four good hours left to get ready." He escaped out the door.

Thoughtfully, Flanna followed.

Trace headed for the stream but she went on inside the soddy. The dogs, having returned from their field chase, eyed the two of them going off in different directions. Samson, the male, loped after Trace. Delilah stayed with her.

Her one-room home was a cozy place, but as she stepped through the door, the thought struck her it must not appear like much to Trace.

Over time, and because she and her father had built the house themselves, she'd grown accustomed to the single, windowless room. They saved their window money for the new house and when the weather was good did most of their living outdoors. The furnishings were simple but well made — a table, a few chairs, a rocker, and a bed. Her pride and joy was the cast-iron stove that Rory had planned to move to the new house when the time was right.

Taking a pail, she fetched water for washing and then set it on the stove to boil. While waiting for the water to warm, she started a stew for their dinner. As she worked, she decided she was not displeased with matters between herself and Trace. He was doing his best to push her away . . . and yet she didn't think he was succeeding.

God had brought him back into her life for a reason and this time, she'd not let him go. Her gaze fell on the double bed pushed into one corner of the room. A nervous energy stemming from anticipation fluttered in her stomach.

Trace thought her a tease. Yes,

she'd admit part of her father's sales had been her ability to lead men on a wee bit — but not with Trace. Never him. From the first moment she'd laid eyes on him, she'd loved him. Brave, bold, strong — he'd been the epitome of everything she'd dreamed a man could be.

Time had proved her devotion. She'd made a terrible mistake in not staying with him. And yet, in truth, she would have made a miserable sheriff's wife, especially in Loveless. Rory had claimed that the towns-people had been the easiest marks of his career because of their puffed sense of importance. She was not surprised they hadn't treated Trace right.

Still, she had not expected to find him like this. The man she'd known had been full of confidence. For eighteen long months she'd pictured Trace as going on and forgetting about her. After all, there'd been many a lass eyeing him.

But he hadn't turned to solace in the arms of another. Instead, if her woman's soul read the signs right, he'd been as bereft without her as she was without him.

Flanna placed a lid on the stew pot, ready to move the warmed water off for washing, when she was struck by a revelation. Her eyes strayed again to the bed.

Loveless was not for them. But here, on this blessed parcel of land, she and Trace could make a life for themselves. They could build something of substance. Together.

All she had to do was convince him.

She knew he'd forgive her, but would he give her another chance?

Her first step, she decided, was to show him she had changed . . . and that she'd make a man a fine *wife*.

CHAPTER SIX

Trace drove himself hard to get as much as possible done before dark — and to erase Flanna's disturbing presence from the edges of his mind.

He was too damn aware of her for his own good. She made his blood hot in a way no woman had before or after her. But he would leave her, as soon as he'd taken care of Slayton.

Burned once, he wasn't fool enough to let her close a second time.

He wove the rope through the trees along the other side of the stream. The dog, a mottled-brown male hound with soulful eyes and a wagging tail, followed his every step. Inside the stable, Trace found two bottles from Rory's medicine-show days and hung them in the tree branches close enough together for them to clink quietly when the wind blew. If Slayton sent riders this way, the horses would hear the soft sound and grow skittish . . . or so Trace hoped.

He loaded the lumber for the house into the wagon and then pulled it himself to a point halfway up the bluff. The dog tagged along, his tongue hanging loose.

Trace's plan was to make a make-shift barrier by stacking the lumber much like a split-rail fence below the bluffs crest. Slayton's riders would charge over the bluff and then be surprised. With a spade, he started digging into the hard earth to make a posthole to bury a footing.

"I brought you water," Flanna's

voice said from behind him. He turned and his breath caught in his throat. She'd braided her hair in a single plait that hung over one shoulder. The simple style made her look younger, vulnerable, except for where the tip of the braid brushed the crest of her breast.

His imagination leaped to a picture of her without the calico dress, with them alone, together. At one time his body had burned for her to the point his nights had been restless.

Now, as she dipped a ladle into the pail of fresh water, he wondered what she would do if he gave in to temptation and ran his hand along her clean, shining hair to the wayward tip of that braid.

"This is from the spring," she said, unaware of the lust drumming in his veins. "It's the sweetest water you can imagine."

He grunted an answer, not trusting his voice, and tried to focus on anything but the curl resting on her breast. He was all too conscious of his own disheveled state. Lifting the ladle, he drank his fill. The water seemed to spread through his body, renewing him . . . and slowly, he let down his guard . . . just a little.

After all, this was Flanna. At one time he'd shared his dreams with her.

If she noticed a change in his stance toward her, she gave no indication. "I washed your shirt and hung it to dry."

He was conscious the shirt he was now wearing was filthy. "Thank you."

Almost shyly, she said, "I found a rip in the sleeve. I sewed it."

He nodded. This conversation about mundane things seemed intimate — like the sort of inconsequential conversation between a husband and a wife.

Abruptly he backed away from the direction of his thoughts and picked up the shovel. "Thanks for the water."

She didn't leave. He dug into the earth, giving her his back.

"Do you think that running a rope through the trees will be enough?" she asked.

"It's the best we can do with what we have."

"I'll help you dig," she offered.

"I'm fine, Flanna. Go back to your house."

"It's no trouble. The stew is on and there is an hour or two before dark. We can get more done if we work together. I'll fetch another shovel." Before he could protest, she'd set down her pail and run down to the stable. The dogs loped along beside her.

Trace swore under his breath. Stubborn. She was the most irritating woman —

He dug his shovel into the earth, pushing it deep. If she thought he'd coddle her, she was wrong. He set a plank of wood in the shallow hole he'd dug and measured the distance for the next hole.

"Here we are," Flanna said, coming up the bluff carrying a short-handled spade. "What do you want me to do? Dig a shallow hole like you did this one?"

He didn't want her to do anything, and he would have told her so — except when he looked up, the words died in his throat. She stood, ready and willing with those two mixed-breed dogs flopped at her feet and happily panting. He tempered his words. "Yes. Like I am."

She nodded and set to work. As he stacked a set of "rails" on top of the other, she said, "Now I see. There's no trick here. Together, we'll have this done in no time."

Her attitude in the face of Slayton's attack was cheerful. Trace didn't know what to make of her, so he tried to ignore her.

But no such luck.

"Did I tell you the dogs' names?"

He wasn't interested.

"Samson and Delilah," she said as if he'd asked. "They're brother and sister, of course, but we thought the names fitting."

Delilah. Figures. He kept his opinion to himself but as she started sharing with him more details of her and Rory's dreams for the ranch, he couldn't help listening.

Finally she asked a question he had to answer. "This barricade we're building won't be hurting the horses, will it? I wouldn't want that on my conscience even if the animals are being ridden by the worst sort of pigs imaginable."

He smiled at her summation of Slayton's men. Flanna never held back her opinion. "I've thought of the horses, too. They'll be surprised but they should manage fine. Besides, the rails aren't nailed. They will topple off each other."

"Spook the horses and break the necks of their riders!" she finished in triumph. In spite of himself, a rusty chuckle escaped. It had been so long since he'd laughed, the sound almost startled him.

Flanna seemed to sense it, too. A quick, satisfied grin crossed her face before she changed the subject.

"We're almost done here since we're about out of wood. What shall you do with the ground we can't cover?"

"I'm not worried. Slayton's men will take the easy way, depending on speed for their attack. This should catch them. If they try the way of the barn, the animals will tip us off. I'll roll the wagon over by the house and stand watch there. We should be ready for them tonight."

"I can stand watch, too."

He wasn't about to let that happen.

Women were to be protected, not to be protectors, but he'd not voice his opinion because he knew Flanna would argue. Instead he said, "Maybe."

She wiped her hands on her skirt. "There's not much daylight left. I'd best check on my stew. You come down as soon as you're finished and I'll have a hot meal for you."

A hot meal. The smell of cooking meat wafted from the stove stack to where Trace stood. It had been a long time since he'd had a home-cooked meal. "Do you have any soap?"

She lifted her shovel handle up to rest on her shoulder. "I do," she said with cocky humor.

"I could use a bit."

Her smile lit her face. "It's scented with Attar of Roses, not eau de lilies."

He caught her joke, and managed a crooked smile. "I don't suppose it would do me any harm."

She laughed, the sound as light as the wind skittering across water. "No, no harm at all. I'll fetch it." She headed toward the barn to deposit her shovel.

Trace watched her come out and then walk toward the soddy. The dogs trailed her heels, probably hoping for their dinner.

The sun was setting and everything was bathed in a mellow, golden light. Even the humble soddy appeared grander than it was and in spite of Slayton, of the danger . . . for the first time in a long while, Trace felt a sense of peace.

Flanna watched Trace sit quietly

across the table from her, sipping his coffee, and realized how homey this scene was. The dogs rested on a rug before the stove.

When he walked in for dinner, clean, shaved, his hair slicked back, his lean, muscular body smelling of roses, well, she'd felt a bit giddy, like a girl meeting her first beau. Every time she glanced at him, she was struck anew at what a fine and brawny man he was. A woman could do far worse.

Through dinner, they'd wisely set aside the past and talked about the weather, the livestock and the search Flanna had made for her fifty head. She was certain Slayton had the animals. The hired hand Rory had brought on to watch the beasts had disappeared right after the shooting.

Trace knew more about ranching and farming than she'd imagined.

However, now, with their stomachs full, a companionable silence stretched between them. She picked up her darning basket, needing something to do with her fingers and to distract her mind.

This was the way it was between married couples. This space of time in the evening when chores were done and dinner finished. If they really were married, they would blow out the lanterns and go to bed together.

For a second Flanna couldn't move. She could barely breathe at the image her mind conjured. Back in Harwood, during their kiss, she'd felt him, bold and hard.

He wanted her.

And, God save her, she wanted him, too.

In spite of their vagabond existence, Rory had been an overprotective father. He'd not let anyone dally with his daughter and she'd not wanted to — until she'd met Trace. Now the fact that the two of them were alone fueled her imagination. Her inattention cost. Accidentally she stabbed herself with the needle. Raising her finger to her lips, she sucked the prick, lifting her gaze to see if he noticed — and then froze.

Trace was sound asleep. He sat upright in his chair, his hand resting loosely curved around the tin coffee mug on the table.

She set her darning aside and rose quietly. Moving around to the back of his chair, she gave in to temptation a moment and curled one strand of his hair around her fingers. "You need a haircut," she whispered and then placed a hand on his shoulder. He didn't move. The man was exhausted and who could blame him after the drinking, the fight, the trial and almost hanging? He'd not be happy he'd fallen asleep. He'd interpret his need for sleep as a sign of weakness . . . and yet to her it made him endearingly human. This was the side of him she liked best.

"Come along, Trace," she said in his ear. "It's time for bed."

He mumbled something about needing to stand watch.

"Yes," she agreed. "You must stand watch. Here now, come over here."

In his sleep he was as compliant as a

child. She easily directed him the few steps to the bed. "Rest here a moment while I check the horses."

He was so exhausted, he did as she asked.

Flanna looked down at him and her heart filled with her love of him. Rory's rifle rested in a corner, loaded and ready. She picked it up and with a soft command to the dogs to follow, went outside to take a post in the wagon to watch for Slayton.

Trace woke with a start. He'd been dreaming that he had to stand watch and when he woke, he was disoriented.

Slowly he took in his surroundings: the earth walls, the thin wood floor and the smells of coffee and the meal he'd shared with Flanna. The soddy he'd disdained when he'd first seen it had turned out to be a warm, hospitable *home*. He was in bed, comfortable and cozy.

But Flanna. Where was she?

He said her name aloud. No answer. The dogs weren't there, either.

Instantly alert, he sat up. His holster and gun hung from the bedpost. He pulled out his gun and cocked it. His boots were still on his feet but the fire was dying in the stove. He'd been asleep a few hours.

Swiftly, he made his way across the soddy and opened the door. The light of a half moon, bathed the landscape in shadow and silver. All seemed quiet. Samson slept on across the threshold. He wagged his tail in greeting and rose to all fours.

His gun still poised, Trace searched

for some sign of Flanna. He didn't see her. He thought about calling out and decided against it. She shouldn't have let him fall asleep. What if Slayton had come and taken her?

He bit back panic.

"Where is she?" he said in a low voice. To his surprise, Samson answered by taking off toward the wagon. At his approach, Delilah raised her head and Trace knew Flanna was there.

He lowered his gun and hurried toward the wagon, determined to give her a piece of his mind for not waking him. Samson and Delilah both took off in another direction. "You're right," he whispered. "You don't want to hear this." He raised his voice. "Flanna!"

No answer.

His heartbeat kicked up a notch. What if she *wasn't* there? He leaned over the edge of the wagon and found her sound asleep on the hardboard bed.

Relief washed through him.

She must have been as bone-tired as he'd been. Cradling the rifle to her, she slept with the weariness brought on by a day's hard work.

They were damn lucky Slayton hadn't attacked.

Trace glanced around. He saw no movement on the rise of the bluff or in the shadows of the trees around the stream. There was nothing but the call of a night bird and the music of insects. They could be the only two people in the world.

He returned to the house, grabbed the quilt off the bed and then walked back to the wagon. Flanna didn't even wake when he hopped up beside her on the wagon bed. He spread the quilt over her sleeping form and then settled himself beside her, his back against the wagon seat.

For a second he sat quiet. Then, gingerly, he lifted her shoulders and placed her head on his thigh so she might sleep more comfortably. With a soft sigh, she eased deeper into sleep.

He could have carried her inside . . . but he liked being with her this way.

Carefully, reverently, he reached out and stroked the silken length of her braid. Her cheek appeared downy-smooth in the moonlight.

And he faced the truth: he'd never gotten over her. Not really. He'd pretended but she was the only woman he'd ever loved.

Love. Such a small word and, yet, he hadn't been the same since she'd introduced him to its full meaning.

He looked out into the night. Dawn was a few hours away. If Slayton hadn't struck by now, he probably wouldn't until later, but still Trace would be prepared for him. He had to protect Flanna.

In the morning, he'd give her a tongue-lashing for not waking him. But for now, it felt good being this close to her. The terrible emptiness he'd felt when she'd left him back in Loveless eased.

And as he stood guard the rest of the night, he wondered if maybe, just maybe, he should take another chance on Flanna.

That is, if she'd have him.

CHAPTER SEVEN

Flanna woke the next morning with the most wonderful sense of well-being. She'd not slept so hard since before her father's death and Slayton's threats.

With a start, she remembered she was in the wagon and her purpose. She should not have fallen asleep.

She scrambled up and was surprised by the quilt around her shoulders. And she was in bed.

She looked around. Where was Trace? Had Slayton come?

Spring sunshine formed a rectangular pattern on the floor. All was quiet. Her panic was eased by the gut feeling that all would not seem so peaceful if Slayton had attacked.

To punctuate her thoughts, her rooster crowed and there was a meadowlark's trill as if in answer. Lambert, the rooster, always strutted and crowed midmorning. The day was well advanced. She'd slept late.

Flipping her sleep-ragged braid back, she put her feet over the edge of the bed. Trace must have removed her shoes. She had a hole in the sock right over her big toe and her dress was hopelessly wrinkled. Trace couldn't be more furious with her than she was with herself. How could she fall asleep during her watch?

At that moment, as if she had conjured him, Trace appeared in the doorway. His tall, broad-shouldered frame blocked the welcoming sunlight.

She came to her feet, covering one

foot self-consciously with the other to hide the hole. "I know what you are thinking and I was wrong, wrong, *wrong* not to have woken you. And then to have fallen asleep myself! I'm so blessed sorry and I won't let anything like that happen again —" She would have continued verbally flogging herself but he held up a hand for quiet.

"Slayton didn't come and no harm done. You didn't do anything wrong. Besides, you must have needed the sleep." He paused, his gaze studying her face, then followed the line of her neck, lingering over her breasts and down all the way to her toes. Her heart beat a funny little trip.

"You look more rested," he said. There was a warmth in his voice that made her toes curl.

"I am," she answered, her voice suddenly a husky squeak. She turned, needing to give herself respite from those silver eyes of his that seemed to see everything. He walked into the soddy, his bold, masculine presence filling the room . . . and she found it hard to breathe.

Uncertain, she touched her braid. What had she seen in the depths of his eyes? Want? Hunger?

No, something more. Something she'd thought never to see again. So filled with astonishment was she, she dared not put a word to it — yet.

He moved toward the stove. "You were so tired, I made biscuits and you didn't even move. Not even when they were baking."

She could single out the scent of biscuits now that he mentioned them.

134

"You made them?"

"And gravy." He opened the lid of her iron skillet. "It's not fancy but it's pretty tasty."

Her stomach growled in response.

For a moment she was paralyzed with embarrassment. Their gazes met . . . and then they both laughed, relaxed again.

"Here, I'll dish you up some grub," he said, and reached for a heavy china plate from the pinewood cupboard beside the stove.

Flanna took the moments of his inattention to unplait her hair. She ran her brush through it and decided to leave it be for the moment. Then she pulled on her sturdy shoes.

When she walked over to the table, she was glad she hadn't rebraided her hair. Trace lifted his hand as if to

135

reach out and touch her — but he stopped. "You have the loveliest hair. I used to dream about it."

She held her breath. "I was in your dreams."

His gaze met hers. He gave the smallest of nods and then abruptly stepped back. "I'd best get outside and stand watch. Wouldn't be good for Slayton to come riding in and me standing here moony-eyed."

Moony-eyed. She loved the sound of those words. Before she could speak, he ducked out the door. Both dogs went with him, easily accepting his leadership in the household.

Flanna sat down at the table, her hunger forgotten. Something had happened overnight. He'd decided to let the past be. There was trust again and on trust, one could build love.

Trace loved her.

She knew it all the way down to her woman's soul. He hadn't said the words, but he was *moony-eyed* and mooney-eyed wasn't far from love.

Rory would have told her himself that when a buyer was interested, you kept the product in front of them. She picked up her plate, grabbed a fork, and headed outside to be with Trace.

Trace sat on the wagon seat, the rifle across his lap, alert and watchful for signs of Slayton. But he was also aware of the woman inside the soddy. He knew the moment she stepped out the door.

She walked toward him, her plate in one hand, a fork in the other, and her red-gold hair shining in the morning sun like a bright lure. She'd changed, too, into a practical dress of brown calico. She appeared like the kind of woman a man fought to protect.

The dogs wagged their tails in greeting as Flanna climbed up into the seat and plopped down right beside him. "I was lonely," she explained to his unasked question. "Couldn't see any sense eating inside on a glorious day like today." She dug into a gravy-covered biscuit. Savoring the first bite, she hummed her satisfaction.

Trace watched with a befuddled sense of awe.

"I think the people of Loveless were foolish to let you go," she said, taking a piece of biscuit and sopping up the rest of the gravy.

"Because I can cook?" he asked, using humor to guard against what he feared she might not say.

"Because you are the type of man who will take a stand." She added, "And you know what you're doing. Trust me, Burrell Slayton is quaking in his boots." She said the last with relish and he had to smile.

Then he turned serious. "The truth is, I never did fit in Loveless."

"But you were born there."

He shrugged. He'd assumed someone had told her.

"Why is that?" she asked softly. "You were always standoffish but I thought it was because you were sheriff. Was there another reason?"

He studied the line of the bluff, watchful for the appearance of movement, but his mind was on her question. Then, with feigned nonchalance, he said, "My mother was the local whore. Loveless used to know wild days. Some folks have long memories."

He waited, anticipating her reaction with a touch of dread. During his last days in Loveless, his long-dead mother's line of work had been the buzz of gossips.

"Rory had to run from Ireland because he stole a pig from the magistrate," she said. "My mother was the youngest of ten daughters of a Catholic farmer who didn't have an acre of land to his name. She thought her chances for a good life were better with a pig thief than her family."

"Did Rory ever try and not take anything that wasn't nailed down?" Trace asked, relieved that she hadn't withdrawn after his small confession.

"No," Flanna said simply, and then laughed. "I never knew my mother.

She caught a chill in Missouri and died while I was still a babe. I'm lucky Rory didn't leave me with some farmer's family. He was a rascal, but I loved him. Did you get along with your mother?"

Trace considered the question. No one had ever asked him about her before in a normal, everyday sort of way. "Yes. She was a good woman and she did what she had to do to survive. She raised me right."

"But you never knew your father?"

"She never talked about him." He leaned forward, warming to the subject. "When I was a kid I used to ask questions. I know she got pregnant and her family threw her out, but that's about all . . . and eventually, that got to be enough."

Flanna set the plate aside and slid a

few inches closer to him. Her thigh brushed his . . . and she hooked her hand in the crook of his arm.

He sat still. The wind ruffled her hair as she looked over to the stream. She smelled of sunshine and woman — a woman he loved. What had been between them once had never died.

"All of this, even down to the scrawniest chicken, is because of you," she said.

"I drove you out of Loveless."

She leaned closer. "Ah, yes, but you also made me want *more*." She paused. "Don't you want more, Trace? Or were you thinking of drifting the rest of your life?"

Was she asking him to stay? To help build the house over by the stream with the big porch to enjoy during the evenings?

He could see himself there, raising the walls . . . creating a home.

"You know, Flanna, Rory was right about me. I really am not good enough for you."

She smiled, not looking at him, and said quietly, "You're all I ever wanted."

For a second Trace feared his ears played tricks but then she swung toward him and, there, in the depths of her eyes was the truth. She loved him!

And in her love was power. Loneliness, anger, regret, doubts — all fell away from him. Flanna Kennedy, this wondrous, mercurial woman, loved *him*. He wrapped his arm around her —

Samson sat up and barked. Delilah quickly joined him. They jumped off the wagon and ran toward the barricade blocking the path over the bluff. Trace lifted the rifle, ready to fire.

"Get down," he ordered, "as close under the seat as you can."

Of course she didn't obey him. "Hand me your gun."

"And let you shoot off your toe? Get down." He pushed her off the seat and, with a hand on her head, forced her to follow his orders.

A wagon drove over the bluff. "Hello!" the driver yelled, and then reined in when he saw the barricade. "Flanna? It's Jacob Gustaf."

Flanna's head popped up. "It's my neighbor." She climbed backward out of the wagon. Waving, she started up the hill toward Mr. Gustaf.

With a soft oath, Trace followed, keeping his rifle at the ready.

Mr. Gustaf was a tall, long-nosed

man dressed in somber clothes. He nodded at Trace but turned his attention to Flanna. "I've come to warn you, Miss Kennedy, Slayton is planning to come out here and burn you to the ground, but I can see by the fence you already know."

"We're surprised he hasn't shown up yet," she said bitterly.

Gustaf sent a nervous glance in Trace's direction. "There are some who don't want to battle Mr. Cordell. He has a reputation. Slayton's having trouble rounding up a party of men. But he plans on coming out here tonight."

"How many men has he gathered?" Trace asked Gustaf.

"Not many. Even Judge Rigby isn't falling into line." Gustaf's gaze drifted down to the rifle in Trace's arms. He shifted nervously. "I came to take Miss Kennedy to my place. She'd be better off there."

"You're right," Trace agreed, and would have put her up in the wagon next to Gustaf but Flanna stepped back.

"I'm not going to run. I'll stay here and fight."

"Flanna —"

"I won't go, Trace. You could tie me up and put me in Mr. Gustaf's wagon and I'd escape and run back."

"Miss Kennedy, this land isn't worth your life," Gustaf said.

"This land is my home," Flanna countered. "I won't leave."

Trace couldn't blame her. He looked up at Gustaf. "Can you fetch the U.S. marshal? He's in Dodge. Then we can stop a man like Slayton for good."

Gustaf shook his head. "I don't know. I've got two sons, a wife. Slayton would destroy my farm. Look what he did to Rory Kennedy."

Flanna placed her hand on Gustaf's wagon. "I understand. It's not your fight."

But Trace didn't understand. This was the way it had been back in Loveless. They'd wanted him to fight the dirty battles, but once the town was clean, they'd expected him to leave.

"Then, get on your way," he told Gustaf coldly. "Tomorrow evening come around. We'll either be here or we'll not. If we're here, you won't ever have to worry about claim jumpers like Slayton again."

"I wish . . ." Gustaf started but then hung his head. "I wanted you to be warned."

Trace answered, "I'll be waiting for him."

"*We'll* be waiting for him," Flanna corrected. "Goodbye, Mr. Gustaf."

The man didn't like leaving. Trace could understand. He'd not like admitting he was a coward, either.

They watched the wagon turn and drive out of sight.

Trace broke the silence. "You should have gone. I could have handled this by myself."

"You've always been by yourself." She linked her fingers in his. "I left you once. I'll not leave you again."

He felt humbled in the face of her love. "Flanna Kennedy, will you marry me?"

"Yes, Trace. Yes, yes, yesyesyes!"

For a second he could barely believe his good fortune. With a whoop of joy, he lifted her in his arms and twirled her around. The dogs barked, wanting to join in the play.

Then Trace lost his footing. They both tumbled to the ground, laughing, he protecting her fall with his body, the rifle on the ground beside them.

Flanna looked down at him, her body stretched along his.

The laughter stopped as they both became aware of how intimately they fit together.

He reached up and ran his hand along her bright, shining hair. He wanted her so much. He wanted to brand her with his body, with his love.

"We'll marry tomorrow," he promised, then added with a smile, "We'll have Rigby say the words since he likes to talk so much."

"Tomorrow," she agreed softly. Again he ran his hand over her gleaming hair, burying his fingers in the curling mass. Dear God, he wanted her, wanted her as he'd never wanted another woman before.

"Tomorrow, we may not be alive," she said soberly.

"I'll not let anything happen to you," he swore fiercely. He'd fight with a superhuman strength to protect her.

She placed a finger over his lips. Her legs were entwined with his. He could feel the beat of her heart against his chest, its rhythm mingling with his own. "Whatever happens, we'll be together. But I'm not going to wait for some pompous fool like Rigby to say vows before I make you mine."

She smiled, her eyes shiny but serious. "Will you, Trace Cordell, take me to be your lawful wife?"

CHAPTER EIGHT

Trace sat up, causing Flanna to straddle him, her skirts hiked up, her knees on either side of his hips. "Flanna, are you sure?"

She knew what he was asking. She trained her gaze on his and continued, "To love and cherish. To hold fast in your heart through sickness and in health."

The dogs, stretched out on the grass, watched with lazy curiosity. A bird flitted to the wagon seat and cocked its head. Even Bill, Trace's gelding, and her Spice had wandered over to the fence to witness.

He took her hands in his. "I do. Do you, Flanna Kennedy, promise to love, honor —" a smile came to his lips "— and *obey* me?"

She laughed. "I shall love, honor, and listen to you the best I can," she vowed.

His teeth flashed white in his smile. Then he added soberly, "Till death do us part?"

"Yes." She pulled her hands from his and cupped the sides of his square jaw. His skin was warm beneath her touch. "Forever."

"Forever," he echoed.

For the space of several heartbeats, in which she could have sworn neither one of them breathed, they stared at each other, caught up in the miracle of their love. "Yes," she confirmed aloud, "this is a miracle. I thought you were lost to me and here we are."

"Husband and wife," he said. In

one smooth movement he rose to his feet, carrying her with him. His arms supported her as he walked down the bluff toward the soddy.

Flanna clung to him, her arms around his neck. This was right. This was the way it should be. But Trace walked right by her small house. Instead he carried her to the wood house. He stepped onto the first floor, the frame of the walls all around them.

"Wait for me," he said, and headed off to the soddy. A moment later he came out carrying the cotton mattress and quilts. He spread the mattress out on the floor and threw the blankets over it.

"I don't want us to be together in that dank soddy," he explained. "I'd rather have the fresh air and cottonwood trees for a roof. After we beat Slayton, we'll build this house and this ranch into the finest in all Kansas."

She stepped into his arms. "I love you."

Pride lit his silvery eyes. "I love you." Then he kissed her. This kiss was different than the one yesterday. This kiss held promises, commitments.

Flanna opened herself to him, her heart pounding in her chest. When his tongue first touched hers, she started but then relaxed. This was Trace. This was her husband. She knew any vows she took on the morrow would pale in comparison to these vows of her heart.

Trace started undressing her.

Samson and Delilah, sensing they

were not wanted, jogged off to chase rabbits. Above in the trees and around the prairie, the birds sang but it was as if they'd created a wondrous choir just for Flanna and Trace.

Without modesty, she held her arms up and he pulled her calico over her head. He tossed the dress aside.

Flanna held her breath. Her nipples pressed against the thin material of her chemise. He began untying the tapes of her petticoats. His lips brushed her breasts, wetting the thin cotton material. She buried her hands in his thick curls, bringing him to her.

For a second she allowed the sensations to overwhelm her and then her petticoats fell to the ground. He bent, his arms around her knees and gently lowered her to the mattress.

Swiftly, intently, he undressed her until she was gloriously naked in front of him — and completely unashamed.

"You're beautiful," he whispered.

"Come to me." She held out her arms.

Trace undressed. He was hard and ready. She discovered her first glimpse at a boldly naked man did not alarm her. Instead she was ready for this. She'd waited for him.

He lay down beside her and pulled the quilts up over them. "If Slayton comes now, he'll be in for a surprise." His arms hugged her close to the heat of his body. "But I could not stop myself for any reason in the world."

"I know," she agreed, and then gasped as he kissed the hollow of her shoulder. He nibbled the line of her neck and circled her ear with his tongue.

"I want this to be good for you," he whispered in her ear.

"It will be." Beneath the covers, she ran her hand up the velvety length of his shaft, pleased with the low growl of desire she drew from him.

His teeth teased her skin, followed by the smooth caress of his tongue. Soft intakes of breath, small sighs, and loving laughter revealed their progress. Each moment seemed to drive the need Flanna felt for him.

At last, he gave her breast one lingering kiss and then settled himself between her legs. He rested his weight on his arms.

"I want this to be good for you," he said, his expression intent.

Instinctively she cradled his body,

her legs around his hips. "It will be."

He smiled. Then, in one smooth movement, he entered her.

Flanna tensed. He stopped, letting her grow accustomed to him. He pressed forward.

There was small pain as he broke through the barrier of her virginity but it was not unpleasant. He was watching her, a line of worry between his eyes.

She soothed that small line with the tips of her fingers, and arched herself up to him. Her movement buried him deeper. Her muscles clenched and then embraced . . . and she was in heaven.

"Dear God, Flanna. You are so tight, so sweet." Trace began moving.

She had thought them done. Now

she discovered there was more, much, much more.

He took his time, paying attention to her pleasure. And, proudly, she met him every step of the way. His thrusts grew more demanding. She didn't know what to expect. A part of her centered on him and another part was spiraling out of control.

Then she discovered where they were going. One moment she was grounded to him and in the next, she was no longer a creature of this earth. She was like the water that bubbled over the rocks in the stream near where they lay. She was music and art and beauty.

Trace knew where she was. He'd been the one to bring her here. Now he thrust once, twice, and then with a glad cry, he filled her. He completed her.

They lay in each other's arms lost in the aftermath of their lovemaking for what seemed like hours. Flanna stroked his arm, admiring the muscle beneath. "Is it always like this?"

"It's never been like this." He looked down at her. He was still inside, connected with her. "We are one." There was reverence in his voice.

For the first time Flanna understood the meaning of the phrase. She threw her arms around his neck and laughed with joy.

They made love several times, right there outside beneath the sky. To Flanna, it was as if they'd created their own Garden of Eden. For the space of a few hours, the world was held at bay.

She lost herself in the heady sensation of desire. Her lips tasted his skin. She loved the warmth and scent of his body . . . and in his arms she felt loved and protected.

No matter what the night would bring, she would not regret giving herself to him.

Ever.

She slid her hand down to her belly. They were snuggled under the quilts, the sky and the cottonwoods their canopy. "I could be with child, even now." The thought gave her a powerful sense of satisfaction.

His hand covered hers, his expression darkening. "Flanna, if something happens to me —"

She silenced him with her lips. "Nothing will happen," she said. "They can't get away with killing my father and you, too. A merciful God would never let such a tragedy come to pass."

"Sometimes, God isn't always watching."

"He is now." She rubbed her cheek along his. "He sees us and is pleased. He will be with us tonight."

Trace's answer was to make love to her, again.

However this time, they moved leisurely, savoring their precious moments together. Afterward, they dressed.

The sun was beginning to set and they prepared to wait for Slayton.

As the moon hit the highest point in the sky the bottles tied to the line clinked softly together.

"Shh," Trace cautioned. "Wait."

Flanna nodded, her hands trembling around the Colt's smooth handle. Trace stood, easing the rifle to his shoulder.

They'd placed the dogs in the soddy. Trace hadn't wanted them to warn their attackers.

There was a splash in the stream. Flanna could hear horses breathing — and then object with a snort at finding the rope.

Trace fired and she started firing with him. He'd told her to let off no more than three shots.

She discovered why. She doubted she hit anything but chaos broke out among their attackers. They hadn't been expecting the rope. At least one of Trace's bullets hit and she suspected by the cursing and hollering, others did, as well.

"I'm hit. I'm hit," one man moaned while others shouted for a retreat.

"Get down," Trace warned, and pulled her off the porch of the house, pushing her under the foundation. "Stay here until I call you."

He disappeared into the night as riders charged over the bluff. She could make out their silhouettes and feel the thundering of hooves.

Then the horses hit the barricade. The riders had not noticed it. Horses squealed warnings and skidded to a halt. Riders were unseated. Flanna could hear them holler as they fell.

Then Trace started shooting. This time, there was no free firing, but the systematic crack of a sharp shooter choosing his quarry.

Guns were being fired from the bluff now. Slayton's men were fighting back. What if they saw Trace, standing alone in the moonlight?

Flanna gripped the Colt and climbed out from her haven. She had to get to Trace, to help him.

A second later a pair of strong arms grabbed her from behind.

Trace watched the last man of the attacking party run retreat.

His plan had worked. The cowards had run. Several men were dead. He hoped Slayton was one of their number.

He jumped down from the wagon. Bill and Spice raced around the corral, still worked up over the battle. The dogs barked madly inside the soddy. Even the chickens seemed upset.

"Flanna!" He started toward the

soddy to release Samson and Delilah.

There was no answer.

His hand on the door, he called again.

This time he was answered but not in the way he expected. "She's here," said Slayton. He stepped out of the shadows of the barn. He held Flanna by the hair, a gag around her mouth, and his pistol pressing against the tender skin of her neck.

Trace felt fear. The dogs seemed to sense what was happening. On the other side of the door, they started growling and acting crazy, wanting to be released.

If Slayton noticed, he gave no sign. "I'm sorry you got involved, Cordell," he said. "Hell, I'm sorry matters got so messy tonight. Maybe if you'd both been a bit more quiet, we could have parted company as friends."

"I doubt that," Trace said carefully.

Slayton's mouth crooked into a smile. "Yeah. You're probably right." He sighed. "Well now, I've got to do what I must do."

"Let her go," Trace said.

"Maybe," Slayton answered. "But first, you toss that rifle off to the side."

Flanna moaned her protest, twisting as she did so. Slayton viciously pulled her hair. "Settle down," he warned.

Trace threw the rifle aside. He had no choice.

"Good," Slayton said, and pointed the barrel of his gun toward Trace. "It was nice meeting you, Cordell."

In answer, Trace opened the soddy door. Samson and Delilah shot out of the house like Chinese rockets. Delilah moved toward Flanna but Samson went for Slayton.

Trace dove for his rifle. Slayton released Flanna and fired off a shot at the charging dog, but he missed. Trace's shot didn't. He caught Slayton right in the chest.

The man jerked back. Samson jumped on him, pushing him to the ground. Shaking, Flanna reached for her dog. Trace ran forward. "Samson," he said, lifting Flanna into his arms. The animal obeyed immediately, falling back to his side.

Flanna buried her face in his chest. "You told me to stay. I wanted to help."

He kissed the top of her head and

then kissed her precious nose, her beautiful eyes and her stubborn chin.

She was crying and he could taste her tears. He hugged her close.

"Is he dead?" she asked.

"Yes."

A shudder went through her and then she relaxed in his arms. At the same moment a party of riders came up over the bluff.

Trace pushed Flanna behind him and raised his rifle. Both Samson and Delilah tensed, ready to attack.

A man called out, "Mr. Cordell, Miss Kennedy, it's me — Gustaf! I brought the marshal from Dodge."

Flanna reached down to soothe the dogs. Trace lowered his rifle but still held it ready. The riders made their way around the barricade, their horses stepping over some of the boards that had been knocked down.

A minute later Gustaf, the marshal, and two men rode into the yard. The marshal was a stocky man with a no-nonsense expression.

Flanna lit a lamp and put water on to boil for coffee.

"It looks like a battlefield around here," the marshal said. "Some of Slayton's men ran right into us. I have a group of men a mile or so down the road holding them in custody." He walked over to Slayton's body and then faced Trace. "Guess you better tell me what happened, Sheriff Cordell."

The next day, an overcast one, Flanna and Trace rode to Dodge to give a formal statement at the marshal's office. Trace brought up the belief that Slayton had rustled Kennedy cattle. The marshal promised Slayton's herds would be searched.

Then Trace walked Flanna down to the wooden church in the field at the edge of town. There, the minister heard their vows.

But in Flanna's heart, no promises carried more weight than the ones she and Trace had made to each other the night before. She told him as much as they walked out the church door.

"And what do you think Rory would have said if I hadn't given you a proper ceremony?" he asked, holding the door open for her.

"I think he would have agreed you are the finest, bravest man I know," she answered.

As if in benediction, rays of sunlight burst through the clouds. She slipped her hand into his. "There, see?" she whispered. "Rory is smiling. Come, Mr. Cordell, and take your wife home. We have a house to build."

Trace set his hat on his head at an angle. "Not just a house, love, but the finest spread in all Kansas."

Flanna laughed, filled with the joy of living. Life held endless promise. "Yes, my love, the finest."

Together, they walked back to their wagon and headed home.

About the Author

The *New York Times* and *USA Today* bestselling author of eleven historical romances, **Cathy Maxwell** spends hours sitting in front of her computer pondering the question "Why do people fall in love?" She hasn't found the answer yet, but when she does — move over Dr. Phil! *Flanna and the Lawman* is Maxwell's first Western, a genre this Kansas-raised girl loves. She lives in Virginia with her three children and her husband, Kevin, who drives her crazy in all the very best ways. Fans can find Cathy's web site at:

www.booktalk.com/cmaxwell

We hope you have enjoyed this Large Print book. Other Thorndike, Wheeler or Chivers Press Large Print books are available at your library or directly from the publishers.

For more information about current and upcoming titles, please call or write, without obligation, to:

Publisher
Thorndike Press
295 Kennedy Memorial Drive
Waterville, ME   04901
Tel. (800) 223-1244

Or visit our Web site at:
www.gale.com/thorndike
www.gale.com/wheeler

OR

Chivers Large Print
published by BBC Audiobooks Ltd
St James House, The Square
Lower Bristol Road
Bath BA2 3SB
England
Tel. +44(0) 800 136919
email: bbcaudiobooks@bbc.co.uk
www.bbcaudiobooks.co.uk

All our Large Print titles are designed for easy reading, and all our books are made to last.